The Gold Disc of Coosa

ALSO BY VIRGINIA POUNDS BROWN

Alabama Mounds to Missiles
with Helen Morgan Akens

Alabama Heritage
with Helen Morgan Akens

Mary Gordon Duffee's Sketches of Alabama
with Jane Porter Nabers

Toting the Lead Row:
Ruby Pickens Tartt, Alabama Folklorist
with Laurella Owens

The World of the Southern Indians
with Laurella Owens

Grand Old Days of Birmingham Golf, 1898–1930

Southern Indian Myths and Legends
with Laurella Owens

George Stiggins's Creek Indian History
editor

Winnataska Remembered
with Katherine Price Garmon

Cochula's Journey

Mr. Gillespy of Glen Iris Park:
Journals of James McAdory Gillespy, 1890-1911
co-editor with Matthew L. Lawson

Mother & Me

The Gold Disc of Coosa

VIRGINIA POUNDS BROWN

Drawings by LaNeil Wilson

Junebug Books
Montgomery | Louisville

Junebug Books
P.O. Box 1588
Montgomery, AL 36102

ISBN-13: 978-1-60306-018-9
ISBN-10: 1-60306-018-9

Design by Randall Williams
Printed in the United States of America

This book was originally published in 1975 by
The Strode Publishers, Huntsville, Alabama,
with Library of Congress Catalog Number 75-24616
and ISBN 1-87397-085-3.

For my young friends who first heard the story
and pestered me until I finished it:

David
John
Liz
Laurie
Kelly

Contents

To the Reader

When De Soto came to the area now called Alabama, he encountered in the Coosa River Valley the most extensive Indian civilization of his four-year journey. On July 16, 1540, he was met just outside the city of Coosa with more pomp than the Spaniards were to see in all the rest of their travels through the country. One of De Soto's captains present at the time wrote, "The cacique (king) of Coosa came out to receive De Soto borne in a litter on the shoulders of his principal men, seated on a cushion, and covered with a mantle of marten skins. On his head he wore a diadem of plumes, and he was surrounded by many attendants playing upon flutes and singing. "

The Gold Disc of Coosa tells what happens from the time of that meeting until October 18, 1540, when the Indians finally made a stand against the Spaniards at Maubila. The battle of Maubila was the first important encounter between the Indians and white men in what is now the United States.

Three men traveling with De Soto kept detailed accounts of the journey. A fourth one later interviewed the survivors in Spain and wrote *The Florida of the Incas*. These writings tell about the Indians the Spaniards met along the way: how they looked, how they lived, how they worshipped. So we have the Spanish view of these first Americans. What we do not have is an account by the Indians of their reaction to the Spaniards.

This book attempts to look at the De Soto story from the Indian point of view.

Authorities agree that the Indians De Soto met were the last of the Mound Builders who flourished between 1200 and 1500 A.D. in the Southeast. They also agree that these Indians showed a close kinship with the Aztec and Maya civilizations of Middle America. They do not agree on how these Indians came to the Southeast and what happened to them after De Soto. Some historians think they were the ancestors of the Creeks, Choctaws, and Chickasaws. Others think they never recovered from their encounter with the white man and just disappeared into history.

In this story I have assumed, because of their similarities to the Mexican people, that the Mound Builders of the Southeast knew the legend of Quetzalcoatl, who had promised to return as a white-faced man. When De Soto appeared, they believed at first that he was Quetzalcoatl just as Montezuma believed that Cortez was the returning god.

V. P. B.

Characters in this Book

INDIANS

TALEMICCO (tal-eh-MEE-koh)—peace-loving king of Coosa.

UTINA (oo-TEE-nah)—sixteen-year-old son of Talemicco.

SUKABOO (SUCK-ah-boo)—high priest of Coosa.

LASKO (LASS-koh)—head runner of Coosa.

MOTECK (MOE-teck)—head warrior of Coosa.

CROCE (CROW'sh)—most influential of the wise old men, who holds the beads giving the history of his people.

COCHULA (koh-CHOO-lah)—Utina's sister.

WEHAKA (we-HAH-kah)—interpreter.

TASKALOOSA (TASS-kah-LOO-sah)—giant king of warlike Maubilians and enemy of Talemicco.

CHICA (CHEE-kah)—Taskaloosa's messenger.

QUETZALCOATL (ket-SAHL-koh-AHT'l)—Indian cult hero.

SPANIARDS

HERNANDO DE SOTO (hair-NAHN-doh de SOH-toh)—
leader of the Spanish expedition. Charles V of Spain
conferred on De Soto the title Governor of Cuba
and Adelantado (ah-day-lahn-TAH-doh) of Florida.
Florida in 1540 included most of the United States
and Canada.

Father Segura (she-GOO-rah)—a priest.

VALDEZ (vahl-DEZ)—one of De Soto's captains.

BOTELLO (boh-TELL-oh)—one of De Soto's captains.

RANJEL (ran-JELL)—one of De Soto's captains.

ANIMALS

ACURAH (ah-KOO-rah)—the great stag.

EL CAMPEÓN (el kam-pay-OHN)—De Soto's horse.

The Gold Disc of Coosa

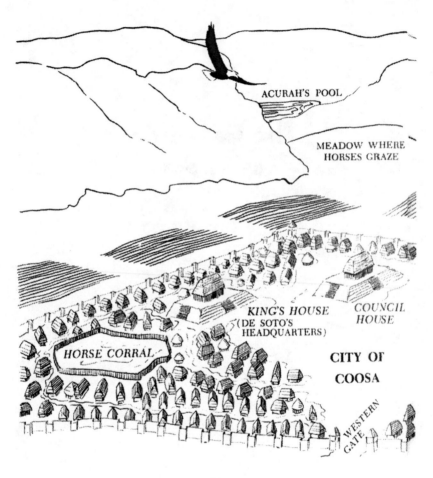

ACURAH'S POOL

MEADOW WHERE
HORSES GRAZE

KING'S HOUSE
(DE SOTO'S
HEADQUARTERS)

COUNCIL
HOUSE

HORSE CORRAL

CITY OF
COOSA

WESTERN
GATE

Map of Coosa

ANCESTRAL CAVE

WHERE UTINA
HIDES EL CAMPEÓN

CORN FIELDS

WHERE UTINA
ESCAPES

GREAT ROAD

MAIN SPANISH ENCAMPMENT

EASTERN GATE

PLAZA

TEMPLE
MOUND

DE SOTO'S ROUTE

ARKANSAS

SOUTH CAROLINA

ALABAMA

COOSA

LOUISIANA

MUSKOGEE

CALUÇA

GEORGIA

MISSISSIPPI

MAUBILA

FLORIDA

TAMPA BAY

De Soto landed at Tampa Bay in May 1539. He had the best equipped force ever to set foot in the New World: 1,000 armed soldiers, 200 horses, 24 priests and monks, thousands of swine, and packs of bloodhounds. Four years later, in May 1542, De Soto was buried in the Mississippi River, never having found the gold he so stubbornly and ruthlessly sought. Of his expedition 311 survivors reached Mexico in 1543.

First Part
Invaded

1

The year was 1540. The midday sun burned hot in the walled City of Coosa. The plaza thronged with people, eager to know what Lasko the runner had told the council about the white-faced ones approaching Coosa.

Silence fell in the plaza when King Talemicco appeared in the doorway of the Council House, his tall headdress of feathers rippling in the hot breeze. The great gold disc, always worn by the kings of Coosa, glistened on his bare chest. Lasko stood on one side of Talemicco and his son Utina on the other. Talemicco raised his arms in salute to the people, but he did not speak as they had expected. Instead he swiftly descended the steps and swept across the plaza toward the Temple Mound. Close behind him followed Utina, who had to quicken his step to keep pace with his father. The people fell back to make way for them. Only one woman dared to reach out and touch Utina's arm, asking, "Are the white-faced ones gods? Is Quetzalcoatl returning to his people?"

Utina did not reply. But as he hurried behind Talemicco, he remembered how his mother had told him about Quetzalcoatl and the gold disc shining now on his father's chest.

"When you are the King of Coosa, you will wear it," she had said proudly. But neither his mother nor Utina thought he would wear the disc. The High Priest Sukaboo had other plans for the King's son. And Sukaboo's power rivaled that of the King himself.

Utina followed as Talemicco climbed the steep steps of the Temple Mound. When the King reached the top, he once again raised his arms in salute to the crowd below. Then, shading his eyes from the midday sun, he looked to the east, the way from which the runner had come. With a deep sigh which Utina alone heard, he turned to enter the Temple. When Utina hesitated, Talemicco said, "Sukaboo waits to make the sacrifice. Come."

Utina stepped through the entrance into the dark Temple room. He saw Sukaboo, the light from the Eternal Fire flickering on his naked, painted body. Rancid fumes rose from the fire and sickened him. The chants of the lesser priests beat on his ears like the death drum. When Sukaboo drew the sacrificial knife over the animal in whose blood Talemicco must wash, Utina turned and ran from the Temple.

"I will not be a priest," he said over and over again as he fled down the Temple steps.

Utina recalled the day in his childhood when Sukaboo had hung around his neck a stone pendant with two flying serpents pictured on it. This was the sign of the priestly cult.

Just four moons ago Sukaboo had sent him into the forest to kill the stag Acurah whom Utina loved as a blood brother. Sukaboo might have chosen another youth of sixteen summers for this test of manhood, but it was on Utina's shoulders he had laid the ceremonial deerskin.

Utina remembered the day well. He had stood in the plaza with his father waiting for Sukaboo to start the ceremony. For as long as the old men of Coosa could remember, the beginning of the planting season had been celebrated with the sacrifice of the largest stag in the forest.

"Sukaboo moves with the speed of a turtle." Talemicco turned his head restlessly, his long copper earrings, the finest in Coosa, swinging around his neck. "The people need to be in the fields, preparing the soil for planting the corn."

His father was a patient man; Utina did not think it was concern for the fields that made him speak in this manner, but concern for his own son.

"Do you think Sukaboo will send me to kill the great stag Acurah?" Utina spoke of what weighed on his heart like a grindstone.

"If he does and you do not go, Sukaboo will denounce you before the people. You will become a Temple slave."

"My father, the King, cannot save his own son from Sukaboo?" The words rose bitter in his mouth.

"Utina knows well the law of Coosa. You belong to your mother's people. Sukaboo is your mother's brother. He has the right to claim you for the priest-hood."

"But," Utina reminded his father, "when I stood no higher than your waist, and Sukaboo came to take me from my mother's house to live with the priest, you defied him. You took me to live with you in the King's House."

Utina looked questioningly into his father's deepset eyes. Talemicco's gaze softened as he turned to reply.

"You were too young to live with fire and blood and crazed men. I wished you to be wise in the ways of Coosa. To learn to barter and trade, and to speak wisely in council."

Just then the great drum sounded on top of the mound. High above, Sukaboo appeared wearing a mask made from an eagle head, his face looking out between the upper and lower beaks. Slowly he wound his way down the steps of the mound like a bird in flight, raising and lowering the giant wings strapped on his arms.

A great silence fell on the plaza, the only sound the rattles on Sukaboo's ankles. Utina moved so close to his father that the feathers of his headdress brushed his shoulder. Sukaboo weaved his way in a dance around the plaza, followed by a lesser priest carrying the ceremonial deerskin.

"He sets the stage like a turkey in mating season," Tale-micco muttered.

Sukaboo stopped before Utina and dropped the deerskin upon his shoulders. Between the hooked beaks of the mask Utina saw the evil smile on the priest's face as he said, "Go, Utina, son of the King, and bring back the stag before the moon rises."

Utina knew then it was not the desire of the Sun God that he be chosen, but the plan of Sukaboo. If he failed to kill the stag, his people would denounce him. And Sukaboo could then claim him for the priesthood.

When the sun was low, Utina took his long bow and his quiver of arrows. He wore the ceremonial deerskin so all the inhabitants of Coosa as well as Sukaboo, watching from the Temple Mound, would know he went to fulfill his mission.

If Acurah were not known to my people because of his great size, I could bring back another, he thought as he turned from the Great Road into the forest. Perhaps even now Acurah had gone over the mountain too far to be found. With this hope, Utina approached the spot where two streams made a pool between the rocks. Here the deer came at nightfall to water.

Utina had first seen Acurah at the pool when he was a spotted fawn close by his mother's side. Utina remembered how the doe had frozen at his approach. When he came closer, she leaped into the underbrush; the fawn had not followed her but had stood still on his long legs, watching Utina curiously. For a long time the boy and the fawn watched each other. The doe came out of the brush, smelled her fawn and turned to drink water once again.

From that time on, Acurah and Utina played together in the forest. Even when Acurah became a great-pronged stag, and Utina no longer a boy, they knew and loved each other.

When Utina reached the water hole and Acurah was not there, the heaviness in his heart lifted. He would return to Coosa and tell Sukaboo that Acurah was not to be found. Already the sun was down, but a rosy afterglow filled the sky. Suddenly, Utina saw Acurah's head lifted above the brush, turned toward him. Utina ran down the path away from the deer, but Acurah leaped along beside him. He sniffed the deerskin curiously and then pressed his wet nose against Utina in greeting.

Shouting at him to be gone, Utina pushed the great animal from him. He raised the bow threateningly above his head. Acurah did not move. Utina struck him a hard blow with the bow. The deer was startled but only backed away. The afterglow had faded and the trees were no more than black outlines. The words of Sukaboo echoed in Utina's ears:

"Before the moon rises, bring the great stag to be sacrificed." Utina struck Acurah a harder blow.

At last the deer bounded down the path away from Utina. Slowly Utina fitted an arrow into the bow and drew back the string. Just then Acurah stopped and turned his head to look back at Utina. With a sob Utina threw the bow from him and ran through the trees away from the deer.

Utina returned to Coosa just at sunrise. He went straight to the King's House where Talemicco lay sleeping. He stood over his father and shouted down at him. "I did not kill Acurah. Nor will I bring any other deer to be sacrificed."

Talemicco rose from his mat and looked at his son, standing feet wide apart, before him. He asked, "Do you no longer fear Sukaboo?"

Utina looked away and would not meet his father's gaze. At last he replied, "I fear him still, but I will not kill my blood brother."

"You know the ways of our people. You have defied Sukaboo."

"My people have need of new ways." Utina threw back his head.

Talemicco reached out and put his hands on Utina's shoulders.

"Someday I must choose the one who will come after me. Such a one must know what customs of our people to hold to and what to let go. In the forest Utina touched the beginning of such knowledge."

Because his father had accepted his refusal to kill the deer, the people of Coosa did not turn their backs on Utina. But Sukaboo was enraged. He sent another youth of sixteen summers to kill the largest stag in Coosa. This time Acurah did not escape.

Utina hid in the forest until the pole on which Acurah had been sacrificed no longer stood in the plaza.

After this, Utina's hatred of Sukaboo knew no bounds.

2

Now Utina had once again defied Sukaboo by running from the Temple Mound. But when the high priest appeared atop the mound, Utina joined the people of Coosa in praise of the Sun God. He raised his arms and chanted "Ah-ei-yah," while Sukaboo entreated the Sun God to make Coosa pleasing to the strange ones approaching the city.

Soon Talemicco seated himself on the high platform in the middle of the plaza. He still wore the feathered crown, but Utina noticed the gold disc no longer hung around his neck. Utina wondered about this as he pushed his way through the crowd toward the platform.

Talemicco rose and spoke to the people, his deep voice resounding through the plaza:

"Two moons ago the first runner came with news of the white-faced ones. He said in the lands to the east many bowed down to the strangers as gods but others believed the white-faced ones sought only a yellow metal; when they did not find it, they made slaves of our people. These things the first runner told us.

"Now comes the head runner of Coosa, Lasko, who has seen these strange ones himself. I command him to tell the people of Coosa what he spoke in the Council House."

Lasko bowed low to Talemicco. Then he turned and faced the plaza.

"A mighty horde comes, my people. I have seen it moving like a giant serpent across the land, crawling and twisting over the mountains and through the valleys. "

The people had heard Lasko speak many times, but never before in a voice like this.

"At its head men carry weapons that roar and flash. Behind them come other men with bows that shoot deadly arrows twice the distance of our own. In the rear are many of our people in chains and behind them herds of small animals."

Lasko stopped speaking and took a step forward. "But in the midst of these are creatures such as we have never seen before."

As he spoke, Lasko's eyes widened and his voice faltered. A murmur rose from the plaza, but Talemicco stilled it with a raised hand and said, "Tell what kind of creatures they are, Lasko."

"They are like two creatures in one-half man, half beast. The man part sits atop the beast part, but when they separate the man part is like a man while the beast part is like no other creature. He is not like a deer."

Lasko glanced at Utina as he said this, for Utina had asked in the Council House whether the creature were like a deer. Lasko continued.

"He is larger and his legs are longer than a deer's. His tail reaches almost to the ground and long hair grows from his neck. He has great spirit and fire. Sometimes he beats upon the ground and snorts and tosses his hair on his neck."

"We hear of one called the Adelantado. Is he such a man-beast?" Talemicco asked.

"He is the man-beast to whom all others bow down. The man part wears the finest garments with the longest feather in his headdress. And the beast part is the swiftest and the most spirited."

"Does the runner Lasko believe these white-faced ones are gods?"

"Soon the King can see for himself if the gods come. Before the sun drops behind the western wall, the white-faced ones will enter Coosa."

Lasko fell to his knees, unable to speak further. Talemicco commanded his attendants to care for the exhausted runner.

Following the custom of his people to debate, Talemicco turned first to the warriors gathered on one side of the plaza: "You have heard the words of Lasko. What make you of this force approaching Coosa?"

Their leader Moteck stepped forward clutching a long spear in one hand and a shield covered with feathers in the other. "Coosa is a mighty city, great King, and many people are subject to us. Our granaries are filled with corn, our storehouses piled high with the finest skins. No city has such a plaza as Coosa, nor any other with such a Temple filled with treasures. The riches of Coosa are known far beyond our boundaries."

Moteck moved a step closer to Talemicco and with fire in his voice he continued. "How do we know this force does not come to rob us and enslave us? How do we know that the half-men half-beasts are not evil gods that would destroy us?

You yourself, oh King, when you were a young man, drove out warring people who claimed land that belonged to Coosa. Now our enemies bow down before us." Raising his spear and his shield, Moteck said, "The warriors of Coosa stand ready to defend the city. Command us, and we will march against the white-faced ones. "

Talemicco, his powerful arms folded across his chest, gave no sign that he had heard Moteck's words. He turned to the elders, the wise men of Coosa, grouped on the other side of the plaza. He asked them the same question: "What make you of this force approaching Coosa?"

Croce, wrinkled with age but standing straight as a spear, came forward. He took from his neck a long string of shell beads which told the history of the people of Coosa. Croce fingered each bead, reading the story cut into it as he spoke. "Many moons ago before our people left the Land of the Sunset and crossed the waters, their ruler was a white-faced god-man Quetzalcoatl. He taught our people how to make garments and hangings from birds' feathers and how to make beautiful vessels and ornaments from gold and silver." Croce pointed toward Talemicco. "The great gold disc of the King was made when Quetzalcoatl ruled our people. When our ancestors crossed the big waters, they brought it and other treasures with them."

Croce took a deep breath. "Warlike gods of neighboring peoples hated Quetzalcoatl. They stirred up wars and brought plagues upon his people. Finally they drove Quetzalcoatl from his land. He disappeared on a raft of hissing serpents into the Land of the Sunrise. He promised someday to return as a white god with a bearded face." Croce put the beads around his neck again and, pointing toward the Eastern Gate, he said, "Let us receive this army in peace and bow down to these strange creatures, for gods they may be."

Croce withdrew and the people waited for Talemicco to speak. But the King remained silent, his eyes fixed, staring into space. So quiet was the plaza that Utina could hear, far off, blackbirds cawing in the fields. Never had Coosa known a time like this.

Finally Talemicco rose. "We will receive the white-faced strangers in peace, and I will go to welcome them to the great city of Coosa." Talemicco's voice rang out through the plaza. "Summon my litter bearers. Prepare for me gifts of pearls and pelts of martens. Open the storehouses and make ready a feast to honor those who come."

Talemicco left the Temple Mound and ascended the small mound on which the King's House stood. He beckoned to Utina to join him. He commanded Moteck to make a formation of the warriors before the mound and the wise men of Coosa to form a line up the steps of the mound.

"Utina will be borne with me to greet the strange ones. When I am no more, he will be King of Coosa." Croce, who kept the treasures of the people, handed to him the mantle of turkey feathers worn by Talemicco when he was the young King. As his father placed the same mantle on Utina's shoulders, the plaza sounded with shouts of "Hail Utina, son of Talemicco!"

Four of the strongest and fastest litter bearers appeared at the foot of the King's Mound, and Talemicco and Utina descended the steps to mount the litter.

Utina felt a hand on his shoulder, and his sister Cochula

whispered in his ear. "You will be the first to see the gods. Place this gift at their feet." She slipped into his hands her greatest treasure, a bracelet of pearls set in a wide gold band.

The bearers raised the litter to their shoulders, and amid shouts from the crowd Talemicco and Utina passed through the gates and out of the city. Utina could see Sukaboo watching from high on the Temple Mound.

He cannot claim me now, Utina thought. But he still wished that the white-faced ones who came would cast Sukaboo down lower than the dogs that whined around the Temple sacrifices.

3

Outside the city walls the procession woun along the Great Road leading from Coosa. The warriors, one thousand strong, the long plumes of their head-dresses waving in the hot breeze, marched at the head of the procession. Moteck, a shield of feathers in one hand, a spear in the other, walked in the center of his men. Behind the warriors came the maidens, adorned with necklaces and bracelets and flowers in their hair. Utina, high on the litter, could see Cochula in their midst, her black hair falling to her waist.

Before the litter the trumpeters sounded their horns. Close around Utina and Talemicco the principal men of Coosa held aloft the banners of the King. Behind them lines of people carried baskets filled with gifts.

As Utina rode along the Great Road, he thought of the day the first runner had come with news of a white-faced horde approaching Coosa. He had been measuring seed corn in the storehouse outside the city when the runner sped by. Utina had stopped his work and raced after the runner into the city as did all the other people in the fields. Now, two moons later, he was being borne on the royal litter to greet these strange ones. He was no longer Utina, son of the King, but Utina, heir to the kingdom of Coosa. Talemicco had proclaimed it before all the people in the plaza.

Utina understood at last why his father had him sit with the council. And he had learned many things. He had learned that a man might say one thing and mean another, just as he knew that an eagle might soar over a mountaintop and alight on an imaginary nest to lure the hunter from the real one.

Within a short time Lasko appeared at the litter with a stranger whose skin was as bronzed as his, so Utina knew he did not belong to the strange horde. Lasko said, "This is Wahaka who speaks the tongues both of the Coosa and of the white-faced ones. He has been sent by the Adelantado to greet you, Talemicco, and to bring you to him."

Just then the warriors ahead stopped, and Utina knew they had sighted the approaching force.

"Tell the Honored One I will meet him on the high bluff, where the river bends to the rising sun," Talemicco said.

As soon as the litter was lowered on the bluff, Utina sprang from it to see better. Talemicco restrained him. "You will sit with me and greet the Honored One. The heir of Coosa does not run about."

Mats were unrolled and soft pads placed on them. Talemicco and Utina sat under a canopy of brightly painted deerskins. The King's bodyguard stood behind them.

Baskets were unpacked, the gifts spread on mats around the canopy: bracelets and collars of metals and shells, cloaks of featherwork, pipes and vessels made to look like animals, pearls from the rivers and colored stones from the mountains. Utina placed Cochula's gold bracelet beside him apart from the other gifts.

Suddenly the earth seemed to tremble. Utina heard a noise like thunder coming up the valley. For the first time he saw the strange creatures. They came six abreast, racing at great speed. At the foot of the bluff they stopped-all but one, and this one, who must be the Adelantado, came thundering on at full speed up the bluff. Utina thought he would charge into his father, but he stopped abruptly, so close that froth from his mouth sprayed Talemicco.

At the first sight of these creatures the principal men and the maidens fled toward the river and the bodyguards fell back into the shelter of the trees.

Utina might have fled with the rest if his father had shown the least fear, but Talemicco did not even draw back when the creature towered over him. He only sucked in his breath and watched as the top half of the creature swung to the ground and walked forward. Utina saw then that he was a man, made just as he was except his skin was white and on the lower part of his face grew black hair.

Talemicco, touching the earth with his right hand and bringing it to his head, greeted the white-faced one. He bade Wahaka, the interpreter, speak these words: "I, Talemicco, King of Coosa, come to welcome you to my land. On my right sits my son, Utina, who will be the King after me. Accept these gifts which we have brought in peace. May the Sun God guide you and protect you on your journey."

The white-faced stranger removed his plumed helmet.

With a low bow to Talemicco he replied, "The land of Coosa has been known to me since I left my ships, and the name of Talemicco is great among all the people we have met. I am Hernando De Soto, Governor of Cuba and Adelantado of

Florida, loyal subject of King Charles V of Spain and servant of our Lord and Savior, Jesus Christ."

"The Andelantado is known to me also. For many moons we have waited to receive you." As Talemicco spoke, he held the piercing gaze of his black eyes on De Soto's face.

De Soto pointed down the long valley to the procession uncoiling like a snake. He continued to speak as Wahaka changed his words into the Coosa tongue. "Behold the might of Spain. Never before has such a force set foot in the New World. In the rear are my foot soldiers; next are my lancers." Then, pointing to the other creatures at the foot of the bluff, De Soto said, "These are my captains, the most gallant and bravest of men. They ride the most noble animal known to man—the horse."

The captains came dashing up the bluff and made a display just as De Soto had.

"And this one," De Soto said, drawing close to him the animal he had ridden, "is El Campeón, the noblest horse of all."

At his master's touch the horse arched his neck and moved his head up and down as if he were bowing. Utina knew he had never seen a more majestic animal. He longed to touch his coat, glistening like gold in the sunlight.

Just then a figure clad in a long black robe stepped forward, holding a large cross in front of him.

"This is Father Segura, priest of our Lord and Savior," De Soto said to Talemicco.

Father Segura, who had eyes the color of bluebirds' wings, knelt before Talemicco and addressed him in a tongue like his own. "I have spent many years among your people in the land we call Cuba. There I learned your language. I beseech you, Talemicco, to receive the Adelantado in peace, and no harm will come to the people of Coosa."

Before Talemicco could reply, De Soto ordered the priest away and commanded that a chest of gifts be placed before the King. In it were heavy garments such as the white-faced men wore, bracelets and rings. Talemicco thanked the Spaniard and pointed to the gifts he had brought. At a word from De Soto the captains fell on the gifts as if they were searching for something.

One of the captains, the smallest one, saw Cochula's bracelet. He took it at once to De Soto. At the sight of the gold bracelet, a change came over De Soto's face. His smile vanished. Speaking rapidly to Wahaka the interpreter, he seized the bracelet and thrust it into Talemicco's face. Wahaka's voice trembled as he said, "The Adelantado wishes to know whence comes the bracelet."

"The bracelet is the treasure of my daughter Cochula. It was brought by her ancestors from the land far to the south." Talemicco replied with great calm even though he did not know how the bracelet came to be among the gifts.

How wise my father was, Utina thought, to have removed the great gold disc before he left Coosa. Utina knew also that he should have foreseen the excitement the bracelet would arouse among the strangers. Was it true, after all, that they sought only gold and made slaves of his people?

As De Soto questioned Talemicco about gold in his kingdom, Utina listened; but he could not take his eyes from the horse El Campeón. Never had he seen a creature of such noble bearing or of such fire and spirit. Finally De Soto stepped back and tossed the bracelet to the small captain, Valdez, as if it were of no importance.

Smiling once again, he turned to Utina. "The heir of Coosa, I am sure, knows no more of gold in this land than his father. He does not even look at me. He sees only my horse."

De Soto drew El Campeón close to him and patted his neck. He beckoned to Utina. Slowly Utina came forward. He could feel the eyes of the captain as well as those of his own people on him. His heart pounded and he feared he might fall because of the sudden weakness in his legs.

But with De Soto holding El Campeón by the bridle, Utina raised his hand and dared to put it on the horse's neck. El Campeón quivered and tossed his head, his great eyes flashing. Utina stepped back, but after De Soto quieted the horse he grew bolder and stroked El Campeón's nose as he had seen the Spaniard do. El Campeón stood very still, his ears pricked forward. Then he made a low whinnying sound and nudged Utina on his arm. At this De Soto laughed loudly, throwing his head back so that his beard pointed into the air. He shouted something to his men who laughed also.

Then, holding the bridle, De Soto gestured to Utina that he wished him to ride the horse. He helped Utina on to El Campeón's back and led him around the ring made by the captains. Utina's legs hung from the horse's side; he could not sit as the captains did with their feet braced. He clung with both hands to the long hair on El Campeón's neck to keep from falling off. But gradually his fear left him. He began to feel a strange bond with the animal. When De Soto slipped the bridle over El Campeón's head and put it into his hand,

Utina took it and rode around the ring once more. De Soto came to help him down, but Utina swung one leg over the horse as he had seen the Spaniards do and jumped to the ground.

"Well done, my son," Talemicco said when Utina returned to his father's side. Knowing De Soto could not understand his words, Talemicco continued to speak in a low voice to Utina. "The warriors are now surrounded by hundreds of white-faced men armed with shooting sticks and the great bows of which we have heard."

So interested had Utina been in riding El Campeón that he had failed to see the foot soldiers marching down the valley. Talemicco continued: "Many more men with long spears mounted on these strange creatures wait at the foot of the bluff. To resist such a force would be useless. De Soto has us in his power."

Talemicco turned to De Soto and addressed him in his most courteous manner. "The city of Coosa even now waits to receive the Adelantado. A feast has been prepared. I will lead the procession into the city so that those within the walls will know that the Adelantado comes in peace."

"Let us ride in side by side, King Talemicco," replied De Soto. "When your people see us together they will know there is peace between us."

Once again Utina mounted the litter with his father, and they were carried back to Coosa. But instead of the royal bodyguard surrounding the litter, there were mounted soldiers whose armor rattled as they rode and whose long spears reached to the sky in a threatening way. Utina did not know what had happened to the warriors or to his sister Cochula.

In such a manner did the procession return to Coosa. What the future held for his people Utina did not know, but he did know that the white-faced ones were not gods but creatures such as he.

4

Never had such a feast been prepared in Coosa as De Soto and his captains ate that first night in the King's House. They fell on the food like starving dogs. Spread on mats before them were platters of deer, turkey, fish, and sweet corn cakes. When these were devoured, the King's attendants served them baskets filled with fresh fruits, berries, and melons.

The Spaniards sat on cushions facing Talemicco and Utina while they feasted. The interpreter Wahaka stood close to Talemicco. Next to De Soto sat the small captain Valdez with Cochula's bracelet hanging from his belt.

"Talemicco sets a king's table," De Soto loosened his belt and wiped his beard. "My captains and I will occupy the King's House while we rest in Coosa."

Utina knew half of the army had entered the city and now occupied all the houses around the plaza. A place had been made for the captains' horses just outside the King's House, and Utina had seen them being fed and watered. The other half of the army remained outside the gates and spread down the valley. The storehouses had been forced open and emptied to feed the Spaniards.

After De Soto had eaten, he began to talk almost faster than Wahaka could interpret. First he told of his country beyond the great waters. It was a land of mountains and valleys like Coosa, but in it were cities larger and richer than Coosa. The King of his land, said De Soto, possessed a fleet of ships that made Spain the mightiest country in the world. De Soto told how he had sailed once before across the great waters to a land to the south where a people called the Incas lived. There he had found great treasures. He had returned to Spain almost as rich as the King himself.

"Now," De Soto said, "I have come to your land seeking a place richer than that of the Incas. When I find this place, I will live in it and rule over it. For twelve moons I have searched. All through the land, I have been told by your people, is gold. They have told me to go east to find it, and in the east they have told me to go west. I grow weary, and my men grow restless." De Soto rested his hand on his sword as he talked to Talemicco. "Some say Coosa is the land we seek."

"Coosa is the richest of lands and our valley the most fertile," Talemicco replied. "We have received the Adelantado as a brother, and we entreat you to stay with us."

De Soto removed his hand from his sword. "Tell me, Talemicco, if my brother you are, is there gold in Coosa?"

Utina had seen the chains ill concealed by the soldiers entering the city, and he knew the fate of those who had displeased De Soto on his journey. He prayed that the Sun God himself would direct his father's reply.

"Alas, we have no gold to offer you. The golden corn

of Coosa is our treasure," Talemicco said. "If it is gold you seek, you will find it in the land south of Coosa in the city of Maubila."

De Soto leaned forward. "Maubila? I have not heard of gold beyond Coosa. Nor of a city called Maubila."

"A great river divides it from other lands. In Maubila sheets of gold line the temple walls." Talemicco spoke in his quietest voice, as if he were holding a council meeting.

"Have you seen this temple?" De Soto asked.

"No. But the principal men of Maubila come to trade in our marketplace, and they tell of it."

A great silence fell in the room. Utina listened in disbelief, for never had he heard of gold in the land south of Coosa. But the King of Maubila he knew well. He was his father's sworn enemy.

Suddenly De Soto sprang to his feet, his hands on his hips, his feet spread wide. "Does Talemicco think to rid himself of his honored guests with such tales? Your people have sought to deceive me since I first set foot on this treacherous land."

Talemicco rose. Never had Utina seen him more commanding. With a flourish the King threw from his shoulders the mantle of marten skins. Utina saw shining on his father's bare chest the gold disc of Coosa, hidden until now by the mantle. At the sight of it De Soto drew back and sucked in his breath.

Talemicco's voice rang through the room as he said, "The King of Maubila gave me this disc of gold as a token of peace between our people." He slipped the disc over his head and dangled it by the chain before De Soto's eyes.

Utina concealed his amazement as he listened to his father.

He watched as De Soto reached out to grasp the disc, but Talemicco drew it away from him. "The incising is the finest and the gold the purest. See how heavy it is." Talemicco now put the disc into De Soto's outstretched hands. The Spaniard balanced the disc in his hands, his fingers closing around it. He raised his eyes and looked sharply at Talemicco. Without lowering his gaze, Talemicco said, "The gold disc is now yours. I give it to you as a token of the peace between us."

Immediately De Soto clamped the edge of the disc between his teeth. Then, smiling, he passed it around for all of the captains to see. Their eyes shone brightly and they laughed and shouted to each other. When the disc came back to him, De Soto said, "Talemicco has honored us with this gift. We will march to Maubila, but first we will rest in Coosa. We desire that you and your son at all times remain in the King's House with us. It is fitting that brothers should be together."

De Soto called his guards and prepared to retire for the night, but Talemicco stopped him. "Always the honored guests of Coosa are entertained with the dances of our maidens. Let them be brought now before you."

Utina was startled at his father's words, for he had not seen Cochula or the dancing girls since they first met the Spaniards outside the city.

"My men are weary," De Soto replied. "Another time we will see the dancers."

"But never have the dancing girls failed to entertain our guests." Talemicco pressed his point.

Utina knew his father was testing De Soto to find out what had been done with the dancing girls. He was afraid De Soto would now throw aside this pretense of friendliness, and that Coosa would be destroyed. But De Soto threw his head into the air, the hair on his chin thrust upward, and laughed loudly. "The captains of Spain will do nothing to offend the maidens of Coosa. I will have the guards bring the dancing girls."

Utina was pleased to see the long dark hair of Cochula among the dancers. They wove their way around the room to the rhythmic sound of rattles on their ankles and wrists. When Cochula came close to him, Utina spoke softly to her. "We are held hostage by De Soto. What is happening in the city?"

"Some of the people are fleeing to the hills. Tonight I will go also."

"Do not go, Cochula," Utina begged her. He remembered the great gray dogs with yellow eyes which the soldiers had brought into the city. "You will be caught."

Before she could reply, the dancers moved away toward the Spaniards. As Cochula danced before Valdez, she caught sight of the pearl bracelet on his belt. Her black eyes flashing fire, she lunged toward Valdez and grabbed at the bracelet, but it would not come free. Angrily Valdez seized Cochula by the arms and threw her to the floor.

Utina sprang to help his sister, but De Soto blocked his way. In one sweep the Spaniard lifted Cochula from the floor. He forced Valdez backward, speaking rapidly to him in a sharp voice.

De Soto released Valdez and stepped back. Slowly Valdez straightened and removed the bracelet from his belt. He threw it at Cochula's feet. She bent to pick it up, her head held high.

De Soto summoned the guards. "Return the dancing maidens to their houses. Take the King of Coosa and his son to their sleeping quarters. Guard them well."

5

The city of Coosa lay like a bird trapped in its own nest. Some of the inhabitants fled to the hills. The Spaniards soon brought them back in chains. After this happened De Soto gave orders for the people to be assembled in the plaza while he stood on the balcony of the King's House with Talemicco and Utina.

At a signal from De Soto, a soldier in the plaza below carrying one of the stick-like weapons set fire to a long thin rope. As the sputtering fire crept toward the stick, he aimed the weapon in the direction of the Temple Mound. Suddenly the noise of thunder came from the stick, smoke filled the air, and a tree limb crashed to the ground at the foot of the mound.

"The Adelantado says he has many more such sticks," Wahaka told the people.

After that most of the people remained in their houses, watching from their doorways the white-faced men and their horses.

While the rest of the city lay quiet and waited, the King's House was busy with the activities of De Soto and his men. Each morning the captains mounted their horses and with

twenty men each left the city. Some rode out the east gate
and some out of the west. Utina knew they went looking for
gold in the mountains.

One day Utina was standing on the balcony watching
the horses below when Valdez rode into the city at full speed.
He rushed into the King's House and slung a pouch from his
shoulder. He emptied the contents before De Soto. "At last,
Capitan General, I have found gold."

Valdez thrust a light-colored rock with small yellow nug-
gets in it before De Soto's face. De Soto took the rock and
turned it in his hand. He pried at a nugget with his dagger
until it loosened. Then he put it on the table and, stroking
his beard, looked at Valdez. "I have thought you a fool before,
Valdez, but now I know it. Have you spent the day digging
this treasure?"

The captain's face reddened. "All day we have dug. The
animals are loaded with the rock."

"I will give you a lesson in gold mining." De Soto stood,
hands on his hips, his chin pointing into the air. "And I do
not think you will forget it. Have your men unpack the cru-
cibles we have carried since we left Spain. Build a fire in the
plaza. We shall see what treasures you have brought from the
mountains."

At De Soto's command, Utina and Talemicco followed
him into the plaza. When the rocks had been crushed and the
fires made, De Soto had Valdez pour the crushed rock into
the crucible. After a time a thin vapor began to rise.

"See, Valdez," De Soto said, "the gold which you bring
becomes a yellow cloud. If you brought true gold, it would
now be separated from the rock and settled in the bottom.

Fool's gold made for fools!" De Soto shouted. "Bring me real gold." He swung on his heels and disappeared into the King's House.

While the Spaniards searched for gold buried in Coosa, Utina dreamed of the horse El Campeón on whose back he had ridden. From the first day the white-faced army had occupied Coosa and Utina had wakened to the neighing of the horses outside the King's House, he had watched the horses. Each morning when the first ray of light crept over the east gate, he slipped to the balcony to look at them in the corral below.

Later, when the horses were driven through the city to graze in the meadow, he gazed after them until they disappeared beyond the gate. And each evening as the sun dropped behind the mountain, he stood on the steps of the King's House listening for the clip-clap of their hoofs on the hard-packed earth as they came back into the city.

One day Utina saw De Soto enter the corral and hold an ear of corn under El Campeón's nose. The horse ate the corn and rubbed his nose on De Soto's shirt. For a long time De Soto stood stroking El Campeón on his neck and talking to him. El Campeón responded with the gentle whinnying noises he had made when Utina petted him.

Utina found an ear of the sweetest corn in Coosa. Before dawn of the next day when he heard the first whimper from the horses, he slipped out and made his way to the corral.

He wondered whether El Campeón would remember him. He seemed different standing in the corral, taller and stronger than when Utina had seen him first. Sensing Utina's presence, the horse pricked up his ears and looked around.

"El Campeón, El Campeón," Utina whispered holding toward him the ear of corn. The horse sniffed it and then nibbled the grain. He nudged Utina's other hand. Utina knew he was looking for another ear. He heard footsteps and dropped to the ground. My nose will be cut from my face, he thought, if I am caught with the Adelantado's horse.

El Campeón only swished his tail as a soldier passed close enough for Utina to touch him. When he had gone, El Campeón lowered his head and with a little whimper nudged Utina gently. Utina dared then to put his arms around the animal's neck and talk softly to him.

Each daybreak after that, while he was sure De Soto still slept, Utina took ears of the tenderest and sweetest corn to El Campeón. If the horse was lying down when Utina came, he quickly got to his feet with a snort. And if Utina was slow to give him the corn, he pawed the ground with one hoof and arched his neck, his great eyes flashing. Utina's wonderment at such an animal grew each day.

One morning Utina reached up and closed one hand on the long hair flowing from El Campeón's neck. He took a deep breath and with one spring leaped onto his back. El Campeón reared once, and then stood still as if waiting to be commanded.

"Someday we will ride down the valley together, O horse of horses." Utina leaned forward over El Campeón's neck until he could whisper in his ear. "Faster than the wind we will ride." Then he slipped to the ground, his heart singing within him, and hurried to the King's House before the guards awakened.

One day, just before the sun was at its highest point, De

Soto had Talemicco and Utina brought into the plaza. They saw standing at the foot of the Temple Mound the cross which the Spanish priest had carried. De Soto and his captains were kneeling before the cross.

Father Segura, a little round cap on the back of his head, spoke to each man and placed something in his mouth.

When the service was over, Father Segura spoke to Talemicco.

"This is the cross on which our Lord and Savior, Christ Jesus, died. This service is a reminder that he died for us." Father Segura looked up at the cross, and a light shone in his blue eyes.

"God raised him from the dead, so that all who believe in him will be saved and have life eternal."

"He was a god-man?" Talemicco asked.

"He was the Son of God. Many moons ago God sent him from heaven to live in a land far away. He taught his people to love one another and to live as brothers."

At these words Talemicco looked at De Soto and his captains and all the soldiers in the plaza, their armor bright in the sun. He did not reply. Father Segura was silent also, his head lowered, his hands clasping the small cross he wore about his neck. At last Talemicco asked :

"Why was he put on the cross and killed?"

"Some people hated him and did not believe he was the Son of God," the priest replied. "We who believe in him are called Christians."

Talemicco studied the cross made from two tree limbs lashed together. Then he gazed searchingly into Father Segura's unflinching eyes. For a long time he did not speak. Finally he said, "In some ways the one of whom you speak is like Quetzalcoatl. He too was a god-man. He came also from his father, the Sun God, to live among us. He taught our people many things, but he too had enemies who drove him from his land and caused him to die. Quetzalcoatl returned to his father, but he promised someday to return."

At that moment the sun came directly overhead. It was the time the people gathered to worship the Sun God. Sukaboo appeared on the Temple Mound and struck the great drum calling the inhabitants to worship. Talemicco and Utina turned toward the Temple, raised their arms in supplication and chanted "Ah-ei-yah," the salutation to the Sun God. The people, not allowed to gather in the plaza, picked up the sound in the doorways of their houses. Soon the whole city rang with the chant.

In the plaza the soldiers seized their lances, and the captains fingered their swords. As the cry grew louder, a look, first of bewilderment and then of alarm, crept over the faces of the Spaniards. Suddenly Valdez drew his sword, waving it in the direction of Talemicco. At the sight of the sword De Soto sprang toward Valdez. He caught the captain's arm and forced the sword down. He spun Valdez around, and beckoning to the captains to follow him, he disappeared into the King's House.

The soldiers lowered their lances. Father Segura, muttering and making signs on his chest, fell to his knees before the cross. And the "Ah-ei-yahs" swelled to a new height, carried by the hot wind from the east.

Second Part

Escape

6

That night as they lay on their mats, Talemicco awakened Utina. "The guards sleep. Go to the temple and tell Sukaboo to do nothing to anger the white-faced army. Tell him not to strike the drum at midday calling the people to worship."

"The salutation to the Sun God will not be said?" Utina could not believe what his father said.

"When De Soto leaves with his army for Maubila, the chant will again be said," Talemicco replied. "Tell Sukaboo the 'Ah-ei-yahs' must now be said silently from the heart, not with the mouth."

"I do not think Sukaboo will heed me," Utina answered.

"Someday you will be the King of Coosa. The mantle has lain on your shoulders. You must learn to speak as the King."

"My voice is not always deep," Utina said. "Sometimes it roars like a mountain cat, but sometimes it trills like a bird."

"I have not chosen you to be the King to roar like a mountain cat." In the darkness Utina felt his father's hand on his arm. "Go to Sukaboo quickly. Warn him of the captain Valdez who longs to shed the blood of our people."

Utina slipped past the sleeping guards into the plaza. The moon shone brightly. He dropped into the shadows of the houses so he could not be seen. He skirted the corral, careful to make no sound lest the horses be disturbed and wake the guards. Crawling behind the Council House to the back of the Temple Mound, he stopped to listen before he began the ascent of the steep steps.

He heard muffled whispering, then the stomp of booted feet descending the steps on the front of the mound. Spanish soldiers, he thought. If they come in my direction I will be caught, for the moon leaves no hiding place.

Utina crouched on the steps, making himself as small as possible. But the footsteps turned toward the King's House. Soon all was quiet again.

Why had the soldiers been on the Temple Mound while the rest of the city slept? Fear drew the skin tight on his head. He started to mount the steps, not rapidly with one great breath as his father did, but slowly and cautiously.

He crawled from one step to the next so he could not be seen in the moonlight by anyone watching from below.

On the top of the mound he made his way to the priests' house. He could see that the mats on which the priests slept were empty. Alarmed, he entered the Temple.

By the light of the Eternal Fire, Utina saw the Temple of the Sun God lying in shambles. The altars had been pulled down, the sacrificial vessels broken. The hangings of featherwork, the pride of his people, had been ripped from the walls and cut into pieces. On the floor in their white sleeping robes lay the priests of Coosa, run through with Spanish lances, their blood still flowing in pools about them. Utina looked at their upturned faces. Sukaboo was not among them.

The scene filled him with such terror he could not move. Valdez has taken his revenge, he thought. Surely now Coosa will be destroyed.

He heard a footstep in the shadows near him. He wanted to turn and run, but he did not know which way to go. He seized a stone from a broken altar and prepared to defend himself. A figure emerged from the shadows and came toward him.

Utina held the rock above his head waiting to bring it crashing down when a voice spoke. "Do not be afraid, Utina."

It was Father Segura, the hood of his long flowing robe pulled close around his face. He carried no weapon. Utina slowly lowered the rock.

"Valdez and his men came to the Temple searching for gold. When they did not find it, Valdez ordered the Temple destroyed. The priests of Coosa threw themselves on the altars to protect them, and the soldiers killed them. God have mercy on them."

Father Segura clutched the cross hanging from his neck.

"Where is Sukaboo?" Utina asked.

"I warned all of the priests of Valdez's approach, but Sukaboo alone escaped into the hills. As soon as the sun rises, the dogs will find him, and he will be brought back in chains."

Utina knew the inhabitants of Coosa would not permit their high priest to be so shamed. Blood would flow in the streets.

"I will bring him back," Utina said. This man talks to me as my own father does, he thought. Maybe he will help me.

Aloud he said, "Help me escape from the city. All know I am the King's son, and the gates are barred to me."

"I will take you at dawn when I go to hold Mass outside the city," replied Father Segura. "You will ride behind me on my horse in the robe of a priest.

"Already the sky in the east lightens. We must go quickly."

Utina took a last look at the dead priests as he stepped over their bodies to leave the Temple.

As they hurried down the steps of the mound, Utina heard shouts from the King's House. He wondered whether his father was safe, and whether he knew of the destruction in the Temple. But Father Segura urged him on.

So it was that Utina once again passed through the city's gates, this time riding, not in the King's litter, but on a Spanish horse and disguised as a Spanish priest.

7

Outside Coosa gray fields were turning gold in the morning light as Father Segura and Utina rode down the Great Road. The priest stopped the horse before they came to the Spanish encampment.

"Keep the cloak close about your face until you are off the road," he cautioned Utina. "The tall corn will conceal you until you reach the shelter of the trees. Hide the cloak on the mountainside."

With a nod of his head, Utina slipped off the horse and disappeared into the field. Father Segura rode on into the encampment.

Beyond the field rose the mountain where Utina knew Sukaboo would be hiding in the great cave of his ancestors. Many times he had climbed to the wide opening, peering into the darkness, feeling the cool air with its dank odor coming from the cave, but he had never ventured into it.

The old men of Coosa told about a Temple Room deep in the cave where the people worshipped when they had first come from their ancestral land. There, spear-like formations made natural altars and steps had been cut into the stone.

Quickly Utina found the path leading up the mountain. He stopped only once when he heard noises rising from the valley. He looked down to see the horses being driven through the gate, along the Great Road and into a meadow. Even at this distance he spotted El Campeón, his coat catching the first rays of the sun.

Utina climbed on rapidly, wondering what would happen in the King's House when De Soto discovered that he had escaped and the people found the priests dead and Sukaboo gone.

Soon the ascent was almost straight up. Utina used his hands and feet to pull himself from rock to rock. As he was almost to the opening of the cave, a figure stepped from behind a boulder squarely in his path. It was Sukaboo, his long white robe torn and dirty, his hair wild about his face.

Utina fell back, too frightened to speak. The skin on his head drew tight, and his tongue stuck to the roof of his mouth.

"The son of the King cannot speak? Are his lips frozen?" Sukaboo, his eyes half closed like a lizard's, looked at Utina.

He is a madman, Utina thought, and he will kill me if I tell him about the priests.

"Your father said to receive this army in peace. Talemicco has the wisdom of a toad." Sukaboo came closer. His eyes fell on the pendant about Utina's neck. He seized it, pulling Utina to him.

"The sign of the priesthood!" Sukaboo stared at the pendant. "Do you know De Soto has dared to send soldiers to the Temple Mound? The white-faced priest warned us so we could escape."

Utina at last found the courage to speak. "You alone escaped. Your priests lie dead, run through with Spanish lances. The Temple has been destroyed."

Sukaboo thrust Utina away from him and, raising his arms, shouted, "The Sun God will be avenged. The streets of Coosa will flow with the blood of the white-faced men."

Remembering that he had promised to bring the priest back, Utina forced himself to face Sukaboo. "For every Spaniard we kill, they will kill one hundred of us. It is our blood that will flow in the streets of Coosa."

"Utina talks with the forked tongue of his father," Sukaboo hissed through his teeth.

Utina slowly edged away from the boulder toward the cave. Sukaboo followed him. Utina stepped backward, into the cave's opening. Taking a deep breath and throwing his voice as low as he could, he said, "I, Utina, in the name of my father, command you to return to the city and to appease the people."

"Utina commands the high priest of Coosa?" Sukaboo laughed, a loud, harsh rasp that echoed into the cave behind him and came back to beat on Utina's ears.

"It is I who command you, Utina, wearer of the serpent pendant, to bring me the horse called El Campeón."

"The horse El Campeón, the one the Adelantado rides?"

"Is he not the finest beast of all, the most perfect one to sacrifice to the Sun God in the Temple Room?" Sukaboo placed his hand on the curved knife stuck in his girdle. "Such a gift will be most pleasing to the Sun God. He will then remove our enemies from Coosa."

"I cannot bring El Campeón to be sacrificed." Utina wondered if Sukaboo knew somehow of his visits to the corral.

"The horse will come with you, and you will bring him to the cave," Sukaboo replied.

"He cannot climb the mountain. El Campeón is not a deer."

"If you lead him up the path, he will climb the mountain."

"But he is not like any other creature. He is the most noble."

"For this reason his blood will be most pleasing to the Sun God," Sukaboo replied. "If you do not bring the horse, I will bring him with the help of the warriors, a spear thrust through his side." Sukaboo smiled at Utina, his red-lidded eyes almost closed.

Even though they were in the cave, Utina stood again in the plaza. He felt Sukaboo place the ceremonial deerskin on his shoulders. He saw Acurah with an arrow piercing his heart.

Now in the cave with Sukaboo watching him, he jerked the pendant from his neck and flung it into the dark opening. He turned and ran from the cave. He did not think Sukaboo would try to stop him.

8

Utina descended the mountain and hid in the low brush near where the horses grazed. He made a gobbling noise like a turkey to attract the attention of the Spaniards guarding the horses, for he knew they hungered for turkey meat. At the sound, the guards picked up their shooting sticks and came toward him. Keeping his body close to the ground so he could not be seen, Utina crept through the brush making more gobbling noises. Slowly, their shooting sticks ready to fire, the soldiers edged toward the woods and away from the horses.

While the Spaniards searched the brush on one side, Utina circled to the other side where El Campeón grazed.

He called softly to the horse. El Campeón raised his head. He called again and El Campeón came trotting toward him. Utina put a halter made from a grapevine around his neck and led him to the woods.

"Sukaboo will not have you," Utina whispered to him as he stepped on the path up the mountainside. "I will take you and hide you. You will be mine."

Utina had gone only a little way when hoofbeats and barking dogs sounded from the Great Road. He looked down to see Valdez dismounting his horse and the foot soldiers with dogs scattering to search the mountainside.

Utina was well ahead of the Spaniards. But as he climbed, the path became steeper. Frequently trees or boulders blocked his way, and he had to lead El Campeón around them. Loose rocks spun from beneath the horse's hoofs and rolled down the mountainside.

Utina was sure the Spaniards had spotted him. He urged the great beast on, pulling at the halter. As if he sensed their desperate plight, El Campeón struggled over the rocks, the great muscles in his flanks straining with the effort, his neck thrust forward.

Well up the mountain, Utina turned from the path leading to the cave toward a rock cliff rising above him. In this cliff a narrow opening led to a mountain meadow. Utina knew this because the great stag Acurah had brought him here.

Quickly, for he could now hear the Spaniards talking as they climbed, he pulled El Campeón through the opening into the natural corral.

"Do not fear." He stroked El Campeón's neck as he wedged the halter between two boulders so the horse could not follow him. Then he scrambled up and over the cliff and down the other side toward the great cave, moving silently and swiftly.

Below, the Spaniards lumbered through the trees, beating the underbrush like the people of Coosa do to frighten the birds from the cornfields.

But not all the Spaniards were so slow. Not the crafty Valdez. He had removed his padded clothing to climb faster, his only armament the dagger swinging at his waist. Utina saw Valdez cautiously climb onto the wide ledge and disappear into the cave. Utina sped down the hillside, giving no thought now to hiding from the soldiers. He must stop the encounter between Valdez and Sukaboo, for he knew each thirsted for the blood of the other.

When Utina entered the cave he could hear nothing but dripping water. Blackness folded around him as if he had no eyes. Groping, he felt his way to the main passage leading to the Temple Room. He had only his hands pressed against the wet walls to guide him. He crawled slowly, expecting to be attacked by Valdez or Sukaboo at every turn.

Gradually the passageway turned downward. No longer was Utina in complete darkness. Light flickered ahead of him. He stood upright and ran down the steps to the Temple Room.

By the light of torches he could see Sukaboo leaning over Valdez. The priest had a deathlike grip around Valdez's neck. Slowly he forced the Spaniard backward so that his chest was exposed. Valdez writhed in pain, flaying his arms and legs. With two swipes of the sacrificial knife, Sukaboo slashed open the Spanish captain. He cut Valdez's heart from his body and laid it on the altar, calling upon the Sun God to be appeased.

For a moment Utina felt his legs sag under him and the scene blurred before his eyes. Never had he seen a human sacrifice before even though he had heard the old men tell of it. Sukaboo will kill me in the same way if he catches me, he thought. He snatched one of the torches and ran back up the passage away from the Temple Room.

Just then he heard the dogs. They had found the entrance

to the cave. If he stayed in the passage, he was trapped, and he did not think he could escape Sukaboo in the Temple Room. Suddenly the barking stopped. The silence was even more frightening than the noise had been. Had the dogs picked up another scent which led them away from the cave?

Then he heard the hard blows of the soldiers on the dogs as they forced them to enter the cave. He lowered himself from the terrace onto which he had climbed and peered down the tunnel toward the cave opening. The dogs had been put on chains, and the soldiers were pulling them into the cave. There was no escape that way. The dogs would be turned loose as soon as they picked up the scent of blood.

Utina's only hope was to find one of the tunnels which he knew from the tales of the old men led out of the cave. By it his mother's family had escaped from their enemies.

He thrust the torch into the mouth of one tunnel only to see it blocked by a large rock. The voices of the Spaniards now sounded louder. Utina knew the light from his torch led them in his direction.

Desperately he swung the torch from one entry-way to the other, looking for the tunnel that led to the outside. When he held it in front of the tunnel with the narrowest entrance, the flame flickered. Somewhere above air entered the cave. Swiftly, he rolled the torch on the damp floor, extinguishing the flame. He squeezed into the tunnel out of the path of the dogs who raced past him barking wildly as they smelled the blood in the Temple Room.

Once again blackness enveloped him as he pushed upward, seeking the opening that must be there. He heard Sukaboo cry out as the dogs reached him. Squirming and twisting, he forced himself on until at last a shaft of light broke the blackness.

In one last effort he lifted himself through the narrow opening out of the cave into fresh air and sunlight.

Even as he had fled for his life, some of him remained suffering with the high priest of Coosa as the Spanish dogs fell upon him. Sukaboo's cries still rang in his ears as he made his way across the mountainside to where El Campeón was hidden.

Utina led the horse down the hillside to the Great Road leading into Coosa. He sprang on his back and spoke into his ear the words that he had promised in the corral. "Horse of horses, we will ride like the wind down the Great Road into Coosa. None will dare stop us."

Utina felt the great beast surge forward at his command, his hands locked in his mane, his legs clasped tightly to his body. They raced past the corn fields and the Spanish encampment through the Eastern Gate. They did not stop until they reached the plaza. "De Soto," Utina called, "El Campeón returns to you."

At his cry De Soto came from the King's House and strode toward Utina. Utina placed the halter in De Soto's hand. Without a word he walked past the Spaniard into the house to seek his father. The captains were strangely silent, turning their backs on him. Talemicco was not sitting in the King's chair.

Utina turned to one of the Spaniards. "Where is my father?" There was no reply.

He turned to run from the house but De Soto stood in the doorway blocking his way.

"Where is my father?" Utina asked again, face to face with De Soto.

"Talemicco strangled the guard who held him when he heard of the destruction of the Temple," De Soto said. "When you did not return, he tried to escape. The captains caught him." Utina paled, and De Soto grasped him by the arm. At his touch, Utina twisted away from De Soto and leaped down the steps into the plaza.

He saw it then, the royal litter at the foot of the Temple Mound. Upon it lay the body of Talemicco, his cloak of marten skins lying at his feet, stained with blood.

Utina fell to his knees. Grief tore at his heart. He would have beat the ground, but he knew De Soto was watching. He rose and walked closer to the litter. Even in death my father is a king, he thought, as he stared at Talemicco's sightless eyes piercing the sky. He took the cloak and covered the torn body. With a steady step, his face set, he walked back across the plaza to where De Soto waited.

"Tonight a new king sleeps in Coosa." He met De Soto's sharp glance as he spoke, careful to show none of the hatred swelling in him. "I will rest on my father's mat."

Third Part
Hostage

9

Three days after the death of Talemicco, De Soto prepared to leave Coosa. His army was rested and well fed. On the last night the Spaniards feasted in the King's House.

"You will go with me," De Soto said to Utina, who had been brought to eat with him and the captains. "You will be carried on a litter as we pass through the land of Coosa. The people will see their King is at peace with me and no harm will come to my army." Utina said nothing, lowering his eyes lest De Soto see the loathing in him.

Slowly the army wound its way out of the Western Gate of the city in the direction of Maubila. It had been almost a whole month since Utina and his father had been borne through the Eastern Gate to greet this same army. The corn had been green in the fields then, the people anxious to greet returning gods.

Utina remembered how the people had hailed him and how proudly he had worn the mantle of turkey feathers. Now the Spaniards had stripped the fields of corn, and many captives had been taken. The King's mantle that De Soto made him wear rested on his shoulders heavy as the chains that bound the warriors and women carrying the Spaniards' burdens on their backs.

A searing heat lay on the land. The Spaniards removed their padded jackets, and the horses had to be watered often. Sometimes De Soto rode close to the litter and tried to talk to Utina. But Utina had no words for him or for any of the captains. He sat erect, his head high, his gaze straight ahead. The only one to whom he spoke was Father Segura, in whose tent he rested at night.

The first night when Utina had lain down, the priest had called his name. Utina had turned his face away and would not reply. The second night Father Segura had approached him with a scroll and a quill pen. "I will teach you the language of your captors," he said. And he drew the likeness of a horse. "Caballo," he said. Utina already knew this word well and scornfully replied, "El Campeón." But each night after that, by the light of a pineknot torch, Utina learned many words.

One night Father Segura drew a figure with the head of an eagle on it. Utina recognized the likeness of Sukaboo. He glanced quickly at Father Segura and saw in the priest's blue eyes the same look he had sometimes seen in his father's eyes. Suddenly he found words to tell Father Segura all that had happened on the mountain above Coosa: the meeting with Sukaboo in the cave, the hiding of El Campeón, the deaths of Valdez and Sukaboo. Utina was able to tell Father Segura even of his grief at finding his father slain. When he had finished, he sat with his hands locked around his knees, his face hidden.

Father Segura knelt by his side and put his hand on Utina's head. "Your father was a peace-loving king, Utina. He tried to save his people. You were trying to do the same."

One moon's march from Coosa, the army came to the wide river that separated the lands of Coosa and Taskaloosa. They camped by the river several days while De Soto's men felled trees and lashed them together into rafts, preparing for the crossing.

On the day of the crossing De Soto stationed Utina on a high bluff above the river. There, surrounded by Spanish guards, he was clearly visible to any of his people who might try to attack the Spanish army scattered along the riverbank.

First to cross were the foot soldiers and the captives. The rafts also carried supplies and swine. Last to cross were the horses and their riders. The horses reared and bucked as the Spaniards struggled to get the frightened animals onto the rafts.

Utina saw De Soto tie a cloth over El Campeon's head before he led him onto the raft. Utina's heart came into his mouth as the raft tilted, and the horse with his heavy trappings lost his footing and almost slid into the water. Utina sprang from the litter, but the guards restrained him. He could only watch as De Soto skillfully maneuvered El Campeón back onto his feet and secured him for the crossing.

Only Utina and his guards now remained on the east bank of the river. De Soto signaled to the bluff as soon as his raft was well away from the shore. Utina felt himself being lifted. He held tightly to the sides of the litter as he was carried down the bluff and onto the remaining raft. Even now, he thought, De Soto protects his crossing of the river by having me on the last raft.

He could feel the eyes of his people watching from their

hiding places in the trees. He was aware that warriors armed with bows and spears had followed the army all through the kingdom of Coosa, moving silently and invisibly. He longed to be rescued, but he knew the warriors dared not attack. At their first move, the lance pricking his back would be driven through him.

When the raft was in midstream, Utina looked back. A band of warriors stood on the bluff, bows at their sides. He could only sit silent, hating De Soto more with every movement of the raft away from Coosa.

On the other side of the river a messenger was waiting to greet De Soto. "The King of Taskaloosa, my master, sends me to salute you. He bids me to say he is told that wherever your path lies you receive gifts and obedience which he knows are all your due, and that he longs to see you."

There was great excitement among the Spaniards from the moment of this contact with Taskaloosa. Utina knew many Spanish words now, and from the captains to the foot soldiers he heard the word "gold" sounding through the air. What will happen, Utina thought, when De Soto finds my father has tricked him?

On the next day Taskaloosa sent word that he would meet De Soto in the city of Caluca. De Soto summoned Utina to his tent that same night. He sat on a couch, feasting on a freshly roasted pig and drinking wine.

"Tomorrow we meet the King of Taskaloosa, and he will lead us to Maubila," De Soto spoke softly. "In Maubila the streets are paved with gold. We know this because your father told us it was so." De Soto, smiling with his mouth but not his eyes, leaned toward Utina. "I will take no more of your silence. Tell me if there is gold in Maubila."

"You have the gold disc from Maubila given to you by
my father." Utina spoke to De Soto for the first time since he
had left Coosa. "The word of my father is honored wherever
men speak."

The Spaniard's eyes narrowed. "We will see the gold together. I will keep you with me all the way to Maubila. We
will march down the streets to the temple filled with gold."

For a brief instant Utina's eyes flickered, betraying his
dismay. He had expected that De Soto would return him to
his people after the army had met Taskaloosa, since he had
no further use for him as a hostage. He had intended to ask
for his sister's freedom. But now he must remain a captive.
With a proud lift of his head he turned to leave the tent, but
De Soto sprang from his couch and swung Utina around to
face him.

"You red-skinned infidel! If you would slip into the forest
some night while the guards sleep, you are free to go. I will
put no chains on the yearling of Coosa." He pushed Utina
away from him. "But when you go, the men of Coosa who
carry our packs and the women of Coosa who entertain us
will run screaming into the forest, their right hands cut from
their arms and their noses cut from their faces."

Utina looked De Soto full in the eye. A noise he did not
know he could make, like the hissing of a snake, came up in
him. Blood rushed into his head, and he could not see. He
longed to take De Soto by his pointed beard and wring his
head from his neck. His arms were strong from using the bow
and the spear. He thought he could have done it before the
guards stopped him.

But he did not. The blood drained from his face. He bowed in the deep salute that his father had given De Soto when he first greeted him. Utina's voice rang sure when he spoke.

"Most honored one, have no fear that I will leave your royal presence. As you and my father were brothers and my sister Cochula is your daughter so are you like a father to me. I will be at your side when you meet Taskaloosa, and I will ride at your side into Maubila. But take no heed of Taskaloosa if he tells you he has no gold. Already he knows what you seek, as we of Coosa knew before you came. Taskaloosa will try to hide his treasure from you."

De Soto speared a bit of pig from the dish before him and ate it before he replied.

"Utina begins to speak with the wisdom of his father. I have not crossed the sea and fought my way through your country to be turned back now."

De Soto put down the dagger and unrolled a long scroll. "This chart marks our journey through the New World. Here is the land of Coosa. When I return to Spain I will tell my King about your fertile valley. And how Talemicco and his son helped me to find gold at last."

The Spaniard continued, "Even now ships wait here to take us back to Spain." Utina's eyes followed De Soto's finger as it moved to a spot south of Coosa. "These ships ride high in the water, but soon they will be loaded with treasures from Maubila. I will return to Spain with more gold than Cortez."

Utina had stood close to De Soto to look at the map spread before him. Between them a grease lamp flickered, casting long shadows on De Soto's face. In no way is he like my father, Utina thought. He is mad like Sukaboo.

Later that night when the moon lay white on the camp, Utina slipped from Father Segura's tent and made his way to where the warriors of Coosa lay chained together. He looked until he found Moteck. Putting his hand over the warrior's mouth so he would not cry out, he whispered, "De Soto holds me hostage until we reach Maubila. If I try to escape he will take revenge on you and the women. But I will help free you. You must take the warriors and the women back to Coosa."

"The warriors of Coosa will not creep away like dogs in the night," Moteck replied. "Even now Taskaloosa sets a trap for the mighty De Soto. At Maubila we will stand and fight, warriors again with bows and spears."

"How do you know this?" Utina asked.

"All of our people know that your father, the King of Coosa, sold us into captivity. But Taskaloosa leads us into battle."

"My father loved his people. He sought peace so that we might live."

"The peoples of Coosa and of Taskaloosa will become one to drive these white-faced ones from our land."

"But the people of Coosa have loved peace. For this reason our corn has been the best and our temples the most beautiful. I will free you, Moteck, and you must return to Coosa with the warriors and the women. De Soto will not delay his march to Maubila to pursue you."

Moteck persisted. "Our fields are laid waste, and our temples are without priests. We have nothing to return to. Talemicco should never have allowed De Soto to enter the gates of Coosa."

"How would you have stopped him, Moteck? Bow and

spear against fire and metal? And what of the captains on horses swinging their swords?"

"The son of the King of Coosa has the heart of an old woman. If you set me free I will go to fight at Maubila."

Utina went back to Father Segura's tent. For a long time he lay awake thinking about the things Moteck had said. He reached out to touch the feathered cloak which De Soto still had him wear so the people would know he was a king. Utina wished his father had never laid the cloak on his shoulders.

10

On the next day, Utina accompanied De Soto into Caluca. Taskaloosa received De Soto in the plaza of the city. The Spanish captains raced in on their horses making a show just as they had done outside Coosa. Taskaloosa, with a canopy of deerskin over him, surrounded by his principal men, watched the display with great gravity.

De Soto approached Taskaloosa who rose to greet him. Utina saw then that Taskaloosa stood at least a head taller than anyone around him. The King looked down on De Soto and said, "The Adelantado is welcomed. With the sight of you I receive a great pleasure as though you were my own brother whom I dearly love. You shall learn how strong and positive is my desire to serve you. Say in what you will command me." De Soto replied with a few words and indicated that he wished Taskaloosa with his attendants to accompany him to Maubila.

The army left Caluca on the following day. At first, as an honor to Taskaloosa, De Soto had him ride on a horse. They traveled in grand style with Taskaloosa's attendants running along beside him trying to keep the canopy of deerskin over Taskaloosa even though he was mounted on a horse. So tall was Taskaloosa that he could find no place for his long legs and finally let them hang like sticks almost touching the ground. Before they had gone far, Taskaloosa told De Soto he would deem it an honor to be carried on the litter in the manner to which he was accustomed.

At noonday, the captain Botello rode up to De Soto at a fast trot shouting, "The captives taken in Caluca have escaped. They cannot be far away. Send me after them. I will bring them back before nightfall."

De Soto agreed for Botello to go, and the captain raced back in the direction from which they had come.

But Botello did not return that night, and De Soto called Utina to his tent at sunrise. "You will go with four lancers to seek Botello and the escaped captives. You will act as guide and interpreter. You will ride Valdez's horse."

He is afraid, Utina thought. He is afraid now to send his captains on dangerous missions. Utina was excited to be riding a horse though he wished it was El Campeón. He had no trouble staying in the saddle and commanding the horse.

With Utina in the lead the lancers made their way back to where Botello had left in search of the captives. Utina spotted the tracks of Botello's horse and followed them into a thicket of trees. There was no sign of Botello, but on a narrow footpath Utina saw bushes crushed to the ground and a tree limb broken over the path. At the sight of this the lancers wished to go no further into the forest, and Utina led them back onto the main road leading into Caluca.

A great stillness lay on the city. The only sound was the clap of the horses' feet. Utina could feel the eyes of the inhabitants watching as they hid in their houses. Utina knew why they had not been greeted when they reached the plaza.

The body of Botello hung from the balcony of the Council House, the flesh so cut they knew him only by bits of his white skin. At the Spaniard's feet lay his horse pierced with arrows and spears. There was no sign of his clothing or his arms. The lancers feared, as Utina did, that a similar fate might come to them. They turned their horses about and raced from the city, stopping only once to rest their mounts before rejoining the army.

When Utina told De Soto of Botello's death, the Adelantado angrily replied, "How dare these heathens defy me!"

"They are trying to frighten us before we reach Maubila and find gold," said one captain.

"Bring the King Taskaloosa to me," De Soto ordered.

Shortly the captain returned. "Taskaloosa says he will receive you in his own quarters."

Taskaloosa is very brave, Utina thought, but he is also very foolish. He has never seen the captains, protected by armor, charging with swords. He has not seen the priests of Coosa laid bare to the bones, their blood spilling over the altars.

"This King does try me above all others," De Soto said. "He must act to protect the treasure at Maubila. But I will go."

De Soto took Utina as his interpreter. Taskaloosa sat on his cushion surrounded by his bodyguard. De Soto told him of Botello's death.

"I must have brought to me the ones who have slain my captain."

Taskaloosa replied that he would send immediately members of his own guard to find the ones who had committed this terrible deed. Since the army was within a few suns' march of

Maubila, the guilty ones would be brought to that city.

"We will also send runners ahead to Maubila to prepare the city for your arrival. My people must bring food and gifts from every part of my land. The white-faced army will be received like gods."

So convincing was Taskaloosa in his speech that De Soto consented for the King's men to leave the army. But, Utina thought, the death of Botello is only the beginning of what lies ahead for the Spaniards. Just as Moteck said, Taskaloosa plans to fight the Spaniards at Maubila. For the first time since his father's death, Utina dared to think of being free again.

Fourth Part

Battle

11

wo moons' march from Coosa, the Spaniards with their captives approached Maubila. The corn in the field had turned brown, and a sharp wind blew from the west. Utina, listening to the wind in the dry leaves, thought of Sukaboo's rattles. He wondered if the women of Coosa had gathered the corn stalks for the winter and if the Spaniards had left any seed corn for the spring planting.

The nearer De Soto came to Maubila the closer he kept Utina by him. But Utina slept still in the tent of Father Segura. At night while the soldiers entertained themselves by the fire, Father Segura continued to teach Utina his language.

One time he pictured the likeness of a great canoe with a tall tree rising from its middle.

"Sailing vessels," he said to Utina. "These will take us back to Spain when we return to the Big Water. You could sail with us. De Soto would be proud to show you to his king."

"Would he take me as a captive, or would his king salute me as my father saluted De Soto? I am now the King of Coosa," Utina replied.

Father Segura dropped his blue eyes. The only sound was the sizzling of the grease burning in the lamp.

The night before De Soto was to enter Maubila, Utina left Father Segura's tent for the last time. He carried the King's mantle with him. Concealed in it was a battle axe which he had taken from Captain Ranjel while he slept.

Utina crept to where the warriors of Coosa lay shackled by the hands and feet. Guards armed with lances and daggers stood nearby. Crawling on his stomach among the resting figures, Utina found Moteck and slipped him the battle axe. "When I signal to you, strike the ankle chains a heavy blow. When all of the warriors have freed their feet, make for the closest woods. We will free your hands there."

Utina crawled away. From a short distance, he hailed the guards in their own tongue.

"Who calls?" one guard asked, for the night was black.

Knowing the Spaniards feared above all the theft of their horses, Utina shouted, "The horses, the horses."

He ran in the direction where the horses were corralled, and the guards followed him. Then he doubled back, hiding behind a tree as the men raced past him.

When Utina signalled, Moteck struck the blow and broke the chains around his feet. More quick, sharp blows and soon each man was free. Silently the warriors crept toward the woods. Utina knew De Soto would not risk sending men in pursuit of captives when he was preparing to enter Maubila the next day.

Utina was the last to reach the shelter of the trees. Moteck had freed himself of his handcuffs and was striking with the axe at the other warriors' chains. "Utina has changed his spots." He looked up questioningly as Utina approached.

"Utina will fight with the warriors of Coosa." Utina spoke

firmly. "We will go to Maubila. Taskaloosa stands against the Spaniards, and we will stand with him. He who was once our enemy is our enemy no more."

Just as the sun rose, Utina and the warriors emerged from the forest. They saw Maubila at a distance. It was a walled city as large as Coosa. But unlike Coosa, it lay on a wide plain, and there were no mountains rising around it.

"The walls are as high as Coosa's," Utina said to Moteck.

"The walls are higher and there are more watchtowers than at Coosa," Moteck replied. "The people of Maubila have prepared for battle. See how they have cleared the plain between the forest and the city." Moteck hurried ahead excitedly. "We can fight with spears and arrows from the walls. The Spaniards will have no place to hide."

As the men of Coosa strode toward the gate leading into Maubila, Moteck instructed the warriors to form a guard around Utina. At last, Utina thought, Moteck accepts me as the King. He draped the mantle around his shoulders and walked proudly in the midst of his warriors.

When they came to the gate, Utina called to the watchtower.

"Open the gate. I am Utina, King of Coosa, escaped from the white-faced force now approaching Maubila. Take me at once to your Council House."

The great doors opened, and Utina and his warriors entered Maubila. They followed the guide through the streets of the city. There are more people here, Utina thought, than ever gather in Coosa, even on the day the corn is traded. But nowhere did he see old women or children. On every side,

working parties prepared for battle. Stones had been lifted to
the top of the wall; stacks of spears rested against the houses.
Utina heard the pounding of poles being fitted into the wall
to make it stronger. He smelled the thick wet mud used to
hold the poles in place. He saw warriors testing their bows
and sharpening their arrows.

Wooden houses lined the streets, and around the plaza
larger houses stood on mounds just as in Coosa. Utina's eyes
brightened at the sight of the Temple on the highest mound.
He could hear his father saying, "Sheets of gold line the Temple
walls." Is De Soto tricked at last? Utina wondered.

When they came to the Council House, Moteck and the
warriors stepped back and Utina entered first. Not only were
the principal men of Maubila present but also the kings of
the lands around Maubila. Already the council was in debate.
Utina recognized the warrior who was speaking; he was Chica,
the messenger Taskaloosa had sent ahead to prepare a welcome
for the Spaniards.

"Taskaloosa says for the women to greet the Adelantado
with music and dancing outside the gates and then to lead
him into the plaza. The warriors must conceal themselves in
the houses so De Soto will not know we plan to fight."

Leaving the Council House, Utina climbed to the top of
the wall to watch the approach of the Spaniards. Long before
the army came in sight Utina saw a cloud of dust and heard the
distant clanging of armor and the neighing of the horses.

First to come on the plain was Taskaloosa, carried on a
litter and surrounded by his bodyguards. Close behind him
rode De Soto and the captains. Following them came about
one hundred foot soldiers and another one hundred mounted

lancers. The main body of the army remained far behind in the woods.

Before the Spaniards reached the gate Utina hurried back to the plaza where he knew Taskaloosa would receive De Soto. Standing well back on the balcony of the Council House where he could not be seen, he watched the procession enter the plaza. De Soto's helmet glistened in the sun, the long plume dancing in the air as El Campeón pranced. Utina's heart leaped when he saw El Campeón; the horse's ears were pricked forward, his coat gleamed gold. At the sight of the horses, the men on the balcony with Utina gasped in astonishment.

Soon the plaza was filled with mounted lancers, foot soldiers and captains. Utina remembered the armed warriors concealed in houses throughout the city waiting to strike. Was it possible that at last these white-faced men would taste their own blood? Taskaloosa has planned well, Utina thought, as the dancing girls came forward offering baskets of food to the Spaniards.

De Soto dismounted. "Take the horses outside the gate," he ordered. Utina saw him look in the direction of the Temple Mound. He longs to race up the steps now to see if there is gold in the Temple, Utina thought.

The litter was lowered, and Taskaloosa stepped down. He pointed out to De Soto the house which the Spaniards were to occupy. Then Taskaloosa strode away from the plaza to the Council House. As he did so, a murmur rose from the captains, but De Soto quieted them. Utina knew that De Soto wanted from Taskaloosa gold, not blood.

Inside the Council House Taskaloosa pushed his way

through the excited warriors, who had left the balcony, to the King's platform.

"The Spaniards have entered our gates." Taskaloosa towered above the assembly as he spoke. "We must wait to attack until the captains are resting in the house and the soldiers have put down their arms to eat. We will fall upon them before they know we have come."

Taskaloosa's eyes swept around the room and came to rest on Utina. "The son of Talemicco, a peace-loving king, joins with his enemies to fight? He no longer sleeps with the Spaniards?"

"I am now the King of Coosa. The bones of my father lie with his ancestors. I have brought my warriors to fight with the white-faced army. They are now my enemy."

No sooner had Utina spoken than shouts were heard from the plaza. Taskaloosa with the other kings hurried to the balcony. They could see De Soto and the captains talking in front of the house prepared for them. Ranjel, at the command of De Soto, walked toward the Council House and called Taskaloosa loudly by name. "Taskaloosa! Taskaloosa!" And then Wahaka, the interpreter, shouted, "De Soto commands you to come out."

Fire flashed from Taskaloosa's eyes as he roared his reply. "Tell the Adelantado that the King of Taskaloosa sits in council. He will come when he has completed his business."

Chica, who carried no arms, walked out of the Council House to give the message to Ranjel.

As soon as Ranjel heard Taskaloosa's words, he seized Chica and cut him open with two slashes of his sword.

At this act, the warriors with a thunderous cry streamed

from the houses around the plaza. They fell on the Spaniards almost before they could draw their swords. Utina felt himself swept along by the warriors to the door of the Council House. Suddenly Moteck appeared at his side, saying, "Stay close by me." He thrust a spear into Utina's hand and a war club into the other.

Utina followed Moteck into the plaza. But the spear and the war club which he had used so well in practice in Coosa felt strangely heavy. His heart pounded so hard that he feared Moteck would hear it even above the noise of the battle.

All was confusion. Utina could no longer see Moteck, only flashing swords and swinging war clubs. He lost his footing and struggled wildly to get up, but bodies pressed down on him. He could not breathe. Suddenly Moteck bent over him and lifted him with one hand, swinging his war club with the other. He dragged him away from the fighting back to the doorway of the Council House.

Then Moteck returned to the battle, pursuing the Spaniards through the gate.

Gradually the trembling left Utina's body, and he tried to sit up. The noise of the battle was far away. In his mind he could still feel feet crushing him down. His breath came in short gasps. He fell back in the doorway, unable to move.

He had used neither the spear nor the war club against the Spaniards. He, the King of Coosa, had been ground into the earth of the plaza. After a while he crawled into the house and hid himself in the darkest corner.

12

Utina did not know how long he stayed cowering in the Council House. He became aware of shouts in the street as the warriors triumphantly returned to the city and were greeted by the women who had remained in the houses during the fighting.

Slowly Utina rose to his feet. He no longer bled from his wounds, but he felt the same kind of pain he had known the day Acurah had been killed. Now I have betrayed my people, he thought. The King of Coosa does indeed have the courage of an old woman.

He saw a figure in the doorway, and Moteck spoke his name. Utina turned his back and would not look at him. Moteck came toward him.

"We have defeated the Spaniards on the plain and taken their supplies. The captives have escaped and entered the city with the Spaniards' treasures.

"I found this in the Adelantado's own packs." Moteck held out the gold disc of the King of Coosa. "Before today you had experienced only the game of war, as you practiced throwing the spear and shooting the bow. In my first battle I was not the brave warrior Moteck. I was the featherless eagle fallen from its nest. I learned the way of fighting. Take the disc."

Utina raised his head to look at Moteck. It was then he saw, noiselessly creeping toward the warrior, a Spanish soldier with a dagger in his hand. Utina opened his mouth to cry out when the soldier, in a running leap, threw himself on Moteck. The warrior turned to meet his assailant, but with an upward thrust the soldier forced the dagger between Moteck's ribs into his heart.

Utina uttered a cry of rage. He seized Moteck's war club and split the Spaniard's skull with a crashing blow. Utina rolled the body of the Spaniard off Moteck and knelt over the warrior. Moteck was dead, one hand still clutching the gold disc.

"No longer is the eagle without feathers, my warrior. May your journey to the land of the Sun God be a happy one."

Utina unfolded Moteck's fingers and took the disc. He slipped it over his head and the gold shone on his chest in the light from the doorway. He thrust Moteck's war club into his belt and slung over his shoulder the bow which Moteck had left standing in the doorway. The smell of blood lay heavy around him. He looked back at Moteck's still body as he passed through the doorway into the street. "At last Utina becomes a warrior," he said aloud.

Shouting and confusion filled the streets. Utina stopped a warrior joyously swinging a captured sword around his head.

"Take me to your King Taskaloosa."

The warrior looked at the gold disc on Utina's chest. "Follow me," he replied.

Taskaloosa was pacing back and forth on the upper walk

of the wall. When he saw Utina, he said, "The mighty De Soto has been driven from our gates."

Utina looked over the wall. Everywhere lay the bodies of the dead and dying. Most of them wore the breech cloth of warriors. Only a bow shot from the wall several hundred warriors formed a line of defense in front of the gate.

"Has De Soto attacked with the horses?" Utina scanned the plain.

"We drove the Spaniards back too fast," replied Taskaloosa. "Even when they reached the horses, they did not have time to mount. They retreated with them in face of our assault."

Just then a great cloud of dust rose from the Spanish line. Utina knew the horses were being readied for battle.

"The Spaniards prepare to attack. The horses will run down the warriors on the plain defending the gate." Even though Taskaloosa towered above him, Utina spoke with authority. "Sound the drum to call the warriors back and close the gate. We must fight from the walls."

Even as Utina spoke, hundreds of horsemen, the sun bright on their lances and helmets, sprinted toward the warriors. The warriors closed ranks and held their shields before them.

Utina looked at Taskaloosa who stood immobile, only his eyes following the advancing horsemen. Utina stepped closer, waiting for Taskaloosa to speak. When he did not, Utina shouted, "Sound the drum before it is too late." Still Taskaloosa watched the plain and did not speak.

Suddenly a mighty roar sounded as the Spaniards charged into the warriors. Only then did Taskaloosa shout for the gate to be closed.

Quickly Utina sprang from the rampart on which he had

stood to a lower walk used by the bowmen shooting through slits in the wall. Slinging Moteck's long bow from his shoulder, he fitted it with an arrow.

The Spaniards had broken through the warriors' line, leaving most of them dead. Now they came on at full swing toward the gate. Utina lined up a horseman and, drawing the bow as far back as he could, he let fly his arrow. The arrow slowed the horseman but did not stop him because of the heavy padded garment he wore.

When the horsemen found the gate closed and arrows flying thick around them, they swung away from the wall and onto the plain again, out of bow shot.

Utina leaped to the upper wall for a better view of the plain. All of the warriors holding the line before the gate had been ridden down by the horsemen. But in the city the people shouted with joy to have turned the enemy from their gate. Utina approached Taskaloosa, still on the wall watching the retreating horsemen, and he warned him once again: "De Soto will be back. He looks for gold in Maubila. When he returns he will bring foot soldiers with axes and pikes to batter down the gate. Only half of his army has even come onto the plain."

Taskaloosa looked down at Utina from his great height. "The King of Coosa knows the Spaniards well. Does he have a plan?"

"We are many in number, like trees in a forest," Utina replied. "But each of them alone is like a great oak. If we could fight them face to face, club to club on this day we could rid our land of the white-faced army. But we have no garments to protect our bodies, no swords or daggers, and no horses.

"What we have to fear most are the horses. Our five thousand will fall before their five hundred if De Soto enters the city with the caballeros and we fight them in the streets."

"What then must be done?" Taskaloosa asked.

"If the Spaniards enter the city we must fight from the houses and from the roof tops. Every blow, every arrow must be carefully aimed," Utina said. "Command the bowmen to send their arrows into the horsemen's faces and into the unprotected part of their bodies." He paused to take a deep breath. "And tell the warriors to get the horses. The Spaniards treasure their horses above all else."

Utina thought of El Campeón as he had last seen him, shining gold, prancing into the plaza. But he thought also of Talemicco and Moteck and the hundreds of warriors dead on the plain.

"We of Coosa are sworn never to be captive again." Utina raised his eyes to Taskaloosa.

"We are as brothers now," Taskaloosa replied. "We also are sworn to fight to death."

13

The city of Maubila waited now for De Soto's next move. There was no joyous shouting in the streets as there had been earlier when the Spaniards had first been turned back. Taskaloosa had heeded Utina's warning and had prepared a battle plan for the Spaniards' next attack.

Shortly after the sun had passed overhead, the lookout on the highest tower shouted down to Taskaloosa on the wall, "The Spaniards have surrounded the city, and foot soldiers are approaching from all directions."

"It has happened as you foretold, Utina," Taskaloosa said between breaths as he shouted orders to his men. "You command the lower walk with the bowmen. I will remain here. The wall must be held."

But the walls of Maubila could not hold back Spanish soldiers protected with helmets and jackets and armed with spikes and axes. Two hundred of them battered down the great gate while hundreds more stormed the walls and swarmed into the city.

Utina fought first with bow and arrow from the wall. Then Taskaloosa gave the order to abandon the wall and to take up arms in the large houses lining the streets of Maubila.

As Utina obeyed the order, he heard the thunder of horses' hooves on the plain. He knew the caballeros raced toward the city and would enter by the fallen gate.

Inside the city, fighting in close combat on foot, the Spaniards had no advantage over the warriors who far outnumbered them. They fell under the blows of war clubs and spears. Some escaped onto the plain.

Utina flayed his war club mercilessly as he moved away from the wall down the street to the plaza. As soon as he reached the Council House he made his way through the hundreds of warriors to the balcony where Taskaloosa watched the progress of the battle.

When he saw Utina, he said, "The streets of Maubila run red with the white man's blood. At last they know the might of King Taskaloosa. I wait for the Adelantado. With my own spear I will impale him upon the Temple wall."

Before Utina could reply, dust billowed up from the gate as the caballeros entered the city. Utina turned and faced Taskaloosa. "Now comes the test of your plan. The men must hold the houses against the horsemen."

When the horsemen found no fighting in the street, only bodies of the dead and wounded, they pulled up their mounts sharply. Then, like a sudden storm, arrows and spears rained down on them from all directions. The horses reared and some were hit. Quickly one of the captains, shouting for the lancers to follow him, turned his mount around and galloped back to safety outside the city.

"They flee like birds before a storm," Taskaloosa said to Utina. "De Soto cannot defeat us."

Utina turned away and did not reply. He thought of the

fallen gate and the battered wall and the hundreds of people in the houses sworn to fight to death. He fingered the gold disc which he still wore. De Soto has not forgotten the gold, he thought.

Once again the city of Maubila waited. Suddenly ten horsemen without weapons raced into the city, swinging firebrands over their heads. Arrows showered on them and seven fell. But the surviving horsemen hurled their burning torches into the thatched roofs of the houses before they could be stopped. One rider, his horse the swiftest, reached the plaza. Utina fitted his arrow and sighted down his bow at the horseman as he charged toward the Council House. Just as the lancer rose in the saddle to throw the firebrand, Utina's arrow pierced his throat. He fell from his horse, but the torch had already left his hand. Instantly flames leaped up from the roof.

The warriors, Utina among them, thronged into the plaza to escape the fire. In every direction people broke through the flames in the houses and poured into the streets. But some did not escape. Utina heard a single cry from the King's House as the burning roof fell and trapped the people within. The fire, fed by a strong wind, soon raged through the whole city.

De Soto himself now led the charge of captains and lancers into the city with foot soldiers close behind. The warriors met them with spears and clubs, the women standing with them. Soon all the fighting centered in the plaza where Spaniards and warriors rolled in waves together, stabbing, thrusting, and slashing. Utina veered away from one lancer who tried to run him through. As the horseman turned to make another thrust at him, Utina threw his war club with such force that

the lancer fell from his horse. Before he could gain his footing, Utina slew him with a Spanish sword he had captured
at the gate.

Suddenly, above the battle roar, Utina heard the scream
of a horse nearby. He knew it was El Campeón. Surrounded
by warriors, De Soto battled desperately near the Temple
Mound. El Campeón was turning and twisting at his master's
command, attacking the warriors with his hooves. Suddenly
an arrow, shot from halfway up the Temple Mound, hit De
Soto in his buttock. He stood straight up in the saddle and
then fell sideways to the ground. Surely now, Utina thought, El
Campeón will be clubbed to death and De Soto with him.

Weaving and darting between rearing horses and battling
figures, Utina sprinted toward the defenseless horse. Just as he
was about to fight his way through the warriors surrounding
De Soto, he saw three captains charge into the circle and force
the warriors back. One dismounted and helped De Soto onto
El Campeón, while the other two held the warriors at bay.
Soon Spanish foot soldiers rushed to form a protective circle
around their wounded leader.

Utina's one thought had been for the fallen horse. He failed
to see a lancer charging from behind who struck a blow to his
head. Utina spun to the ground. He lay face down. Suddenly
the battle seemed far away. He struggled to rise, but a great
weight bound him to the ground. He fell back, the taste of
blood mixed with the dirt of the plaza.

If I am to die, Utina thought, I will die facing my enemy.
With one last effort he came to his knees and turned himself
over. I will not be ground into the earth, he thought. The
sun felt warm on his face, and he thought that he lay again

on the forest floor with Acurah. A long way off he heard a voice like Father Segura's saying, "In the name of our Lord and Savior, spare this one."

And then he knew no more.

14

U tina opened his eyes. A red glow lighted the dark sky. He thought at first it was near day. Was he still lying in the plaza? But what he lay on now was soft and warm, and he was wrapped in it, only his eyes and nose uncovered. Close by he heard moans and pleas for help and the tortured whinnies of wounded horses. He knew then he was in the Spanish camp and the light in the night sky came from the burning city of Maubila. Father Segura must have brought him here and wrapped him in his cloak.

Slowly he raised one hand to his head, feeling the wound from the lance's blow. It no longer bled, but dried blood matted his hair and caked his face. The stench of battle filled his nostrils, and his head throbbed with every heartbeat.

After a while he moved his hand under the cloak, feeling for the disc. It was there.

Utina raised his head. He lay by a pile of brush, a short distance from the Spaniards' camp. Slowly he slid up into a half-sitting position, propping himself on the brush. He saw the Spaniards hurrying in disarray about the camp. By the light from the campfires, he recognized Father Segura moving among the men, kneeling over the wounded and the dying. The soldiers were tearing their padded jackets apart to bind their wounds.

Utina pushed himself up a little higher on the brush. He spotted De Soto half reclining as he was treated for the wound in his buttock. El Campeón stood near him, his head and tail drooped, his ears laid back.

Utina slid back down behind the brush as a figure approached. He felt a cold cloth wiping his face, and a voice whispered, "Utina, it is I, Father Segura."

The cloth helped the pounding in his head, and Utina found strength to ask the question burning in him. "What of my people? Did any escape from Maubila?"

Father Segura put his hand on Utina's arm as he replied, "When they saw they could not escape, they threw themselves into the flames rather than be taken captive."

"Even Taskaloosa?"

"When all hope was gone, he tied a rope around his neck and jumped from the wall. His body hung there for the Spaniards to see as they left the city."

Father Segura looked about him anxiously. "I cannot hide you for long, Utina. I beg of you, go to De Soto. He will need a guide and interpreter. The men want no more conquest for gold. They desire only to return to Spain."

With the priest's cloak drawn close around him, Utina followed Father Segura to where De Soto lay. At the sight of Utina the Spaniard started up but fell back. "The yearling of Coosa who promised me gold in Maubila! For naught have I lost many of my men and scores of horses. Look at my mighty army tonight." His voice was bitter. "Our medicines, our pearls, our sacraments, even our captives, all destroyed in Maubila."

Utina looked down at De Soto's face, blackened by smoke and twisted in pain. He leaned close to the Adelantado before he spoke. "All may not be lost. Gold lies across the Chucagua, the greatest river of all in the land of the Arkansan."

De Soto blinked at Utina from dull eyes. "The son has the guile of the father. Where is this greatest river of all?"

"One moon's march into the west."

"And where is the gold?"

"Another moon's march beyond the river."

De Soto raised himself on his side. Utina saw life return to his eyes.

"I will draw for you on your chart the way to the river and to the gold."

"That chart has been lost in the fire," De Soto replied.

"Then I will burn into a piece of bark the way that you must go."

"You will go with me to lead the way and to be my interpreter," De Soto said.

Utina drew back. "I will not go with you. My life to you is no more than a swipe of your blade. Kill me now, for I will not be your slave." Utina waited for De Soto to order the soldiers to seize him. But he did not.

"The smell of burning flesh sickens me." De Soto looked beyond Utina to the smoldering city. "I do not know who was the victor today. All of your warriors are dead, but they fought valiantly to the end." De Soto beckoned Utina closer. "Return to Coosa." Then he fell back with a deep sigh and closed his eyes

Utina looked at the Adelantado. Did this tortured face once ride with a feathered helmet before a proud army?

Utina turned from De Soto to El Campeón. He drew the horse's drooping head close to him, stroking his neck. Then gently he ran his hands over El Campeon's body, feeling his wounds.

El Campeón trembled, but then he whinnied softly and nudged Utina.

Utina straightened, pulled the cloak around him, and without a backward glance walked beside Father Segura who led him through the camp to the woods.

When the time came to leave the priest, Utina reached out and touched Father Segura's cross.

"When the old men of Coosa tell tales of our people, I will tell of one called Father Segura who came with the white-faced men but was not like other white- faced men. I will tell how he saved Utina from death at the battle of Maubila."

Father Segura raised his hand in a farewell salute.

Utina took a long look at the burning city. "I do not know what has happened to my sister Cochula. If she lives, care for her."

Then he disappeared into the forest.

For three moons Utina made his way back to Coosa. He did not stop to rest the night before he knew he would reach the city on the next day. His heart leaped at the first sight of the mountains, black against the sunrise. When he came to the Great Road leading into Coosa, the weariness left his body. He began to run when he saw the walls of Coosa golden in the early morning light. "It is there," he said aloud, remembering the smoldering ruins of Maubila. In the middle of the Great

Road, he fell on his face praising the Sun God.

Then he sped on through the west gate and through the streets until he reached the plaza. The city still slept. With one great breath Utina ascended the steep steps of the Temple Mound and struck the drum a mighty blow. People came running from their houses to learn why the drum sounded. Utina saw mostly old men, women and sleepy children. Cries of joy arose when they saw Utina. He came down the steps, remembering the day his father had placed the King's mantle on his shoulders. Now he wore the gold disc of the King.

"Our warriors lie buried in the ruins of Maubila," said Utina to his people. "But De Soto at last felt the sting of our arrows and the thrust of our spears. No longer is the Spanish army a mighty serpent creeping over the land." Utina's voice resounded through the plaza. "At Maubila it received a mortal wound. Even now De Soto's love of gold leads him to the great river Chucagua and beyond. But each day his numbers become less. Someday word will come that he is no more."

Utina paused, searching the faces watching him. "If white-faced men come again to our land, we will hide in the mountains. If they find us there, we will die by our own hand, for we will not be enslaved again. Wherever the white man sets his foot, the land bleeds and the waters run red with our blood. So it is sworn."

The people in the plaza echoed, "It is sworn."

"Our Temple is in ruins and our priests dead. We will not rebuild the Temple, and we will kill only to eat, not to sacrifice. This will be most pleasing to the Sun God. Our greatest treasure is still with us. We will plant the golden corn again, and we will live."

Utina turned his back on the people and ascended the mound alone. He looked over the wall to the east just as the sun topped the mountain. He saw again in his mind the Spanish army coming down the Great Road into Coosa, and he heard the hoof beats of the horses. "El Campeón," he whispered as a shaft of morning light through the trees cast a golden shadow on the empty road.

Further Reading

Bernal Diaz del Castillo. **The Discovery and Conquest of Mexico, 1517-1521.** First published, 1632. Farrar, Strauss, and Cudahy, 1965. Spirited first-hand narrative by a Spanish foot soldier of Cortez's conquest of Mexico. Good information on Montezuma, Indian religious rites.

Brown, Virginia Pounds and Akens, Helen Morgan. **Alabama Heritage.** Strode Publishers, 1968. "First Alabamians," pages 1-9.

Ceram, **C. W. The First American.** Harcourt Brace, Josephy, Alvin M., Jr. **The Indian Heritage of America.** Knopf, 1968. "Tribes of the Southeastern United States," pages 99-109. The author speaks of temple mounds built around a large central court or plaza. Also, the Mound Builders' religious rites seem to have their roots in Mexico, according to the author.

Moore, Clarence **B. Certain Aboriginal Remains of the Black Warrior River.** Philadelphia Academy of Natural Sciences, Journal, Vol. 13, Pt. 2, 1905.

Moore, Clarence B. **Moundville Revisited.** Philadelphia Academy of Natural Sciences, Journal, Vol. 13, Pt. 3,

1907. Dr. Moore first systematically excavated Mound-ville in 1905. --

O'Dell, Scott. **The King's Fifth**. Houghton Mifflin, 1966. A novel for young readers of Coronado's search for gold through the Southwest to the fabled cities of Cibola.

Phillips, Philip. **The Maya and Their Neighbors**. University of Utah Press, 1962. First published 1940. "Middle American Influences on the Archaeology of the Southeastern United States," pages 349-374. Phillips concludes that the Mound Builders show "a considerable number of characteristics that can be interpreted as a more or less direct contact with Middle America . . . and those characteristics that gave the culture its special flavor seem to have been introduced directly into the Southeast at a comparatively late time." (pp. 366-367)

Pickett, James A. **History of Alabama**. 1851. "De Soto in Alabama, Georgia, and Mississippi," pages 1-57. This classic work covers in detail De Soto's sojourn in Alabama. Pickett used the original narratives as well as information from Indian sources.

Prescott, William **H. History of the Conquest of Mexico and History of the Conquest of Peru**. First published in 1843 and 1847. Modem Library, no date. These classic works provide invaluable information on Indian civilization in clash with European invaders.

Silverberg, Robert. **Mound Builders of Ancient America: the Archaeology of a Myth**. New York Graphic Society, 1968. Comprehensive survey of the present state of knowledge of all the Indian groups who produced the mounds.

Smith, Buckingham, translator. **Narratives of De Soto in the Conquest of Florida.** Palmetto Books, Gainesville, Florida, 1968.Includes the narratives of the Gentlemen of Elvas and Biedma; also general information on the De Soto expedition in an introduction by Andrew Lytle. The account of the Gentleman of Elvas is strong in capturing the tone and quality of the Indian public speeches. Biedma's account is brief, with exact notations of dates and incidents, e.g., how many horses killed at Maubila, how many men wounded. Both men were part of the De Soto expedition.

CPSIA information can be obtained at www.ICGtesting.com
Printed in the USA
LVOW05s1318021013

355104LV00002B/50/A